The Pig Brother &Other Fables & Stories

Laura E. Richards

The Pig Brother and Other Fables and Stories

The Pig Brother

HERE was once a child who was untidy. He left his books on the floor, and his muddy shoes on the table; he put his fingers in the jam-pots, and spilled ink on his best pinafore; there was really no end to his untidiness.

One day the Tidy Angel came into his nursery.

"This will never do!" said the Angel. "This is really shocking. You must go out and stay with your brother while I set things to rights here."

"I have no brother!" said the child.

"Yes, you have!" said the Angel. "You may not know him, but he will know you. Go out in the garden and watch for him, and he will soon come."

"I don't know what you mean!" said the child; but he went out into the garden and waited.

Presently a squirrel came along, whisking his tail.

"Are you my brother?" asked the child.

The squirrel looked him over carefully.

"Well, I should hope not!" he said. "My fur is neat and smooth, my nest is handsomely made, and in perfect order, and my young ones are properly brought up. Why do you insult me by asking such a question?"

He whisked off, and the child waited.

Presently a wren came hopping by.

"Are you my brother?" asked the child.

"No indeed!" said the wren. "What impertinence! You will find no tidier person than I in the whole garden. Not a feather is out of place, and my eggs are the wonder of all for smoothness and beauty. Brother, indeed!" He hopped off, ruffling his feathers, and the child waited.

By and by a large Tommy Cat came along.

"Are you my brother?" asked the child.

"Go and look at yourself in the glass," said the Tommy Cat haughtily, "and you will have your answer. I have been washing myself in the sun all the morning, while it is clear that no water has come near you for a long time. There are no such creatures as you in my family, I am humbly thankful to say."

He walked on, waving his tail, and the child waited.

Presently a pig came trotting along.

The child did not wish to ask the pig if he were his brother, but the pig did not wait to be asked.

"Hallo, brother!" he grunted.

"I am not your brother!" said the child.

"Oh, yes, you are!" said the pig. "I confess I am not proud of you, but there is no mistaking the members of our family. Come along, and have a good roll in the barnyard! There is some lovely black mud there."

"I don't like to roll in mud!" said the child.

"Tell that to the hens!" said the pig brother. "Look at your hands, and your shoes, and your pinafore! Come along, I say! You may have some of the pig-wash for supper, if there is more than I want."

"I don't want pig-wash!" said the child; and he began to cry.

Just then the Tidy Angel came out.

"I have set everything to rights," she said, "and so it must stay. Now, will you go with the Pig Brother, or will you come back with me, and be a tidy child?"

"With you, with you!" cried the child; and he clung to the Angel's dress.

The Pig Brother grunted.

"Small loss!" he said. "There will be all the more wash for me!" and he trotted on.

THE GOLDEN WINDOWS

LL day long the little boy worked hard, in field and barn and shed, for his people were poor farmers, and could not pay a workman; but at sunset there came an hour that was all his own, for his father had given it to him. Then the boy would go up to the top of a hill and look across at another hill that rose some miles away. On this far hill stood a house with windows of clear gold and diamonds. They shone and blazed so that it made the boy wink to look at them: but after a while the people in the house put up shutters, as it seemed, and then it looked like any common farmhouse. The boy supposed they did this because it was supper-time; and then he would go into the house and have his supper of bread and milk, and so to bed.

One day the boy's father called him and said: "You have been a good boy, and have earned a holiday. Take this day for your own; but remember that God gave it, and try to learn some good thing."

The boy thanked his father and kissed his mother; then he put a piece of bread in his pocket, and started off to find the house with the golden windows.

It was pleasant walking. His bare feet made marks in the white dust, and when he looked back, the footprints seemed to be following him, and making company for him. His shadow, too, kept beside him, and would dance or run with him as he pleased; so it was very cheerful.

By and by he felt hungry; and he sat down by a brown brook that ran through the alder hedge by the roadside, and ate his bread, and drank the clear water. Then he scattered the crumbs for the birds, as his mother had taught him to do, and went on his way.

After a long time he came to a high green hill; and when he had climbed the hill, there was the house on the top; but it seemed that the shutters were up, for he could not see the golden windows. He came up to the house, and then he could well have wept, for the windows were of clear glass, like any others, and there was no gold anywhere about them.

A woman came to the door, and looked kindly at the boy, and asked him what he wanted.

"I saw the golden windows from our hilltop," he said, "and I came to see them, but now they are only glass."

The woman shook her head and laughed.

"We are poor farming people," she said, "and are not likely to have gold about our windows; but glass is better to see through."

She bade the boy sit down on the broad stone step at the door, and brought him a cup of milk and a cake, and bade him rest; then she called her daughter, a child of his own age, and nodded kindly at the two, and went back to her work.

The little girl was barefooted like himself, and wore a brown cotton gown, but her hair was golden like the windows he had seen, and her eyes were blue like the sky at noon. She led the boy about the farm, and showed him her black calf with the white star on its forehead, and he told her about his own at home, which was red like a chestnut, with four white feet. Then when they had eaten an apple together, and so had become friends, the boy asked her about the golden windows. The little girl nodded, and said she knew all about them, only he had mistaken the house.

"You have come quite the wrong way!" she said. "Come with me, and I will show you the house with the golden windows, and then you will see for yourself."

They went to a knoll that rose behind the farmhouse, and as they went the little girl told him that the golden windows could only be seen at a certain hour, about sunset.

"Yes, I know that!" said the boy.

When they reached the top of the knoll, the girl turned and pointed; and there on a hill far away stood a house with windows of clear gold and diamond, just as he had seen them. And when they looked again, the boy saw that it was his own home.

Then he told the little girl that he must go; and he gave her his best pebble, the white one with the red band, that he had carried for a year in his pocket; and she gave him three horse-chestnuts, one red like satin, one spotted, and one white like milk. He kissed her, and promised to come again, but he did not tell her what he had learned; and so he went back down the hill, and the little girl stood in the sunset light and watched him.

The way home was long, and it was dark before the boy reached his father's house; but the lamplight and firelight shone through the windows, making them almost as bright as he had seen them from the hilltop; and when he opened the door, his mother came to kiss him, and his little sister ran to throw her arms about his neck, and his father looked up and smiled from his seat by the fire.

"Have you had a good day?" asked his mother.

Yes, the boy had had a very good day.
"And have you learned anything?" asked his father.
"Yes!" said the boy. "I have learned that our house has windows of gold and diamond."

THE COMING OF THE KING

OME children were at play in their play-ground one day, when a herald rode through the town, blowing a trumpet, and crying aloud, "The King! the King passes by this road to-day. Make ready for the King!"

The children stopped their play, and looked at one another.

"Did you hear that?" they said. "The King is coming. He may look over the wall and see our playground; who knows? We must put it in order."

The playground was sadly dirty, and in the corners were scraps of paper and broken toys, for these were careless children. But now, one brought a hoe, and another a rake, and a third ran to fetch the wheelbarrow from behind the garden gate. They labored hard, till at length all was clean and tidy.

"Now it is clean!" they said; "but we must make it pretty, too, for kings are used to fine things; maybe he would not notice mere cleanness, for he may have it all the time."

Then one brought sweet rushes and strewed them on the ground; and others made garlands of oak leaves and pine tassels and hung them on the walls; and the littlest one pulled marigold buds and threw them all about the playground, "to look like gold," he said.

When all was done the playground was so beautiful that the children stood and looked at it, and clapped their hands with pleasure.

"Let us keep it always like this!" said the littlest one; and the others cried, "Yes! yes! that is what we will do."

They waited all day for the coming of the King, but he never came; only, towards sunset, a man with travel-worn clothes, and a kind, tired face passed along the road, and stopped to look over the wall.

"What a pleasant place!" said the man. "May I come in and rest, dear children?"

The children brought him in gladly, and set him on the seat that they had made out of an old cask. They had covered it with the old red cloak to make it look like a throne, and it made a very good one.

"It is our playground!" they said. "We made it pretty for the King, but he did not come, and now we mean to keep it so for ourselves."

"That is good!" said the man.

"Because we think pretty and clean is nicer than ugly and dirty!" said another.

"That is better!" said the man.

"And for tired people to rest in!" said the littlest one.

"That is best of all!" said the man.

He sat and rested, and looked at the children with such kind eyes that they came about him, and told him all they knew; about the five puppies in the barn, and the thrush's nest with four blue eggs, and the shore where the gold shells grew; and the man nodded and understood all about it.

By and by he asked for a cup of water, and they brought it to him in the best cup, with the gold sprigs on it: then he thanked the children, and rose and went on his way; but before he went he laid his hand on their heads for a moment, and the touch went warm to their hearts.

The children stood by the wall and watched the man as he went slowly along. The sun was setting, and the light fell in long slanting rays across the road.

"He looks so tired!" said one of the children.

"But he was so kind!" said another.

"See!" said the littlest one. "How the sun shines on his hair! it looks like a crown of gold."

SWING SONG

S I swing, as I swing,
Here beneath my mother's wing,
Here beneath my mother's arm,
Never earthly thing can harm.
Up and down, to and fro,
With a steady sweep I go,
Like a swallow on the wing,
As I swing, as I swing.

As I swing, as I swing,
Honey-bee comes murmuring,
Humming softly in my ear,
"Come away with me, my dear!
In the tiger-lily's cup
Sweetest honey we will sup."
Go away, you velvet thing!
I must swing! I must swing!
As I swing, as I swing,
Butterfly comes fluttering,
"Little child, now come away
'Mid the clover-blooms to play;
Clover-blooms are red and white,
Sky is blue and sun is bright.
Why then thus, with folded wing,
Sit and swing, sit and swing?"

As I swing, as I swing,
Oriole comes hovering.
"See my nest in yonder tree!
Little child, come work with me.
Learn to make a perfect nest,
That of all things is the best.
Come! nor longer loitering
Sit and swing, sit and swing!"

As I swing, as I swing,
Though I have not any wing,
Still I would not change with you,

Happiest bird that ever flew.
Butterfly and honey-bee,
Sure 't is you must envy me,
Safe beneath my mother's wing
As I swing, as I swing.

THE GREAT FEAST

NCE the Play Angel came into a nursery where four little children sat on the floor with sad and troubled faces.

"What is the matter, dears?" asked the Play Angel.

"We wanted to have a grand feast!" said the child whose nursery it was.

"Yes, that would be delightful!" said the Play Angel.

"But there is only one cooky!" said the child whose nursery it was.

"And it is a very small cooky!" said the child who was a cousin, and therefore felt a right to speak.

"Not big enough for myself!" said the child whose nursery it was.

The other two children said nothing, because they were not relations; but they looked at the cooky with large eyes, and their mouths went up in the middle and down at the sides.

"Well," said the Play Angel, "suppose we have the feast just the same! I think we can manage it."

She broke the cooky into four pieces, and gave one piece to the littlest child.

"See!" she said. "This is a roast chicken, a Brown Bantam. It is just as brown and crispy as it can be, and there is cranberry sauce on one side, and on the other a little mountain of mashed potato; it must be a volcano, it smokes so. Do you see?"

"Yes!" said the littlest one; and his mouth went down in the middle and up at the corners.

The Play Angel gave a piece to the next child.

"Here," she said, "is a little pie! Outside, as you see, it is brown and crusty, with a wreath of pastry leaves round the edge and 'For You' in the middle; but inside it is all chicken and ham and jelly and hard-boiled eggs. Did ever you see such a pie?"

"Never I did!" said the child.

"Now here," said the Angel to the third child, "is a round cake. *Look* at it! the frosting is half an inch thick, with candied rose-leaves and angelica laid on in true-lovers' knots; and inside there are chopped-up almonds, and raisins, and great slices of citron. It is the prettiest cake I ever saw, and the best."

"So it is I did!" said the third child.

Then the Angel gave the last piece to the child whose nursery it was.

"My dear!" she said. "Just look! Here is an ice-cream rabbit. He is snow-white outside, with eyes of red barley sugar; see his ears, and his little snubby tail! but inside, I *think* you will find him pink. Now, when I clap my hands and count one, two, three, you must eat the feast all up. One—two—three!"

So the children ate the feast all up.

"There!" said the Angel. "Did ever you see such a grand feast?"

"No, never we did!" said all the four children together.

"And there are some crumbs left over," said the Angel. "Come, and we will give them to the brother birds!"

"But you didn't have any!" said the child whose nursery it was.

"Oh, yes!" said the Angel. "I had it all!"

THE OWL AND THE EEL AND
THE WARMING-PAN

The owl and the eel and the warming-pan,They went to call on the soap-fat man.The soap-fat man he was not within:He'd gone for a ride on his rolling-pin.So they all came back by the way of the town,And turned the meeting-house upside down.

THE WHEAT-FIELD

OME children were set to reap in a wheat-field. The wheat was yellow as gold, the sun shone gloriously, and the butterflies flew hither and thither. Some of the children worked better, and some worse; but there was one who ran here and there after the butterflies that fluttered about his head, and sang as he ran.

By and by evening came, and the Angel of the wheat-field called to the children and said, "Come now to the gate, and bring your sheaves with you."

So the children came, bringing their sheaves. Some had great piles, laid close and even, so that they might carry more; some had theirs laid large and loose, so that they looked more than they were; but one, the child that had run to and fro after the butterflies, came empty-handed.

The Angel said to this child, "Where are your sheaves?"

The child hung his head. "I do not know!" he said. "I had some, but I have lost them, I know not how."

"None enter here without sheaves," said the Angel.

"I know that," said the child. "But I thought I would like to see the place where the others were going; besides, they would not let me leave them."

Then all the other children cried out together. One said, "Dear Angel, let him in! In the morning I was sick, and this child came and played with me, and showed me the butterflies, and I forgot my pain. Also, he gave me one of his sheaves, and I would give it to him again, but I cannot tell it now from my own."

Another said, "Dear Angel, let him in! At noon the sun beat on my head so fiercely that I fainted and fell down like one dead; and this child came running by, and when he saw me he brought water to revive me, and then he showed me the butterflies, and was so glad and merry that my strength returned; to me also he gave one of his sheaves, and I would give it to him again, but it is so like my own that I cannot tell it."

And a third said, "Just now, as evening was coming, I was weary and sad, and had so few sheaves that it seemed hardly worth my while to go on working; but this child comforted me, and showed me the butterflies, and gave me of his sheaves. Look! it may be that this was his; and yet I cannot tell, it is so like my own."

And all the children said, "We also had sheaves of him, dear Angel; let him in, we pray you!"

The Angel smiled, and reached his hand inside the gate and brought out a pile of sheaves; it was not large, but the glory of the sun was on it, so that it seemed to lighten the whole field.

"Here are his sheaves!" said the Angel. "They are known and counted, every one." And he said to the child, "Lead the way in!"

ABOUT ANGELS

OTHER," said the child; "are there really angels?"

"The Good Book says so," said the mother.

"Yes," said the child; "I have seen the picture. But did you ever see one, mother?"

"I think I have," said the mother; "but she was not dressed like the picture."

"I am going to find one!" said the child. "I am going to run along the road, miles, and miles, and miles, until I find an angel."

"That will be a good plan!" said the mother. "And I will go with you, for you are too little to run far alone."

"I am not little any more!" said the child. "I have trousers; I am big."

"So you are!" said the mother. "I forgot. But it is a fine day, and I should like the walk."

"But you walk so slowly, with your lame foot."

"I can walk faster than you think!" said the mother.

So they started, the child leaping and running, and the mother stepping out so bravely with her lame foot that the child soon forgot about it.

The child danced on ahead, and presently he saw a chariot coming towards him, drawn by prancing white horses. In the chariot sat a splendid lady in velvet and furs, with white plumes waving above her dark hair. As she moved in her seat, she flashed with jewels and gold, but her eyes were brighter than her diamonds.

"Are you an angel?" asked the child, running up beside the chariot.

The lady made no reply, but stared coldly at the child: then she spoke a word to her coachman, and he flicked his whip, and the chariot rolled away swiftly in a cloud of dust, and disappeared.

The dust filled the child's eyes and mouth, and made him choke and sneeze. He gasped for breath, and rubbed his eyes; but presently his mother came up, and wiped away the dust with her blue gingham apron.

"That was not an angel!" said the child.

"No, indeed!" said the mother. "Nothing like one!"

The child danced on again, leaping and running from side to side of the road, and the mother followed as best she might.

By and by the child met a most beautiful maiden, clad in a white dress. Her eyes were like blue stars, and the blushes came and went in her face like roses looking through snow.

"I am sure you must be an angel!" cried the child.

The maiden blushed more sweetly than before. "You dear little child!" she cried. "Some one else said that, only last evening. Do I really look like an angel?"

"You *are* an angel!" said the child.

The maiden took him up in her arms and kissed him, and held him tenderly.

"You are the dearest little thing I ever saw!" she said. "Tell me what makes you think so!" But suddenly her face changed.

"Oh!" she cried. "There he is, coming to meet me! And you have soiled my white dress with your dusty shoes, and pulled my hair all awry. Run away, child, and go home to your mother!"

She set the child down, not unkindly, but so hastily that he stumbled and fell; but she did not see that, for she was hastening forward to meet her lover, who was coming along the road. (Now if the maiden had only known, he thought her twice as lovely with the child in her arms; but she did not know.)

The child lay in the dusty road and sobbed, till his mother came along and picked him up, and wiped away the tears with her blue gingham apron.

"I don't believe that was an angel, after all," he said.

"No!" said the mother. "But she may be one some day. She is young yet."

"I am tired!" said the child. "Will you carry me home, mother?"

"Why, yes!" said the mother. "That is what I came for."

The child put his arms round his mother's neck, and she held him tight and trudged along the road, singing the song he liked best.

Suddenly he looked up in her face.

"Mother," he said; "I don't suppose *you* could be an angel, could you?"

"Oh, what a foolish child!" said the mother. "Who ever heard of an angel in a blue gingham apron?" and she went on singing, and stepped out so bravely on her lame foot that no one would ever have known she was lame.

THE APRON-STRING

NCE upon a time a boy played about the house, running by his mother's side; and as he was very little, his mother tied him to the string of her apron.

"Now," she said, "when you stumble, you can pull yourself up by the apron-string, and so you will not fall."

The boy did that, and all went well, and the mother sang at her work.

By and by the boy grew so tall that his head came above the window-sill; and looking through the window, he saw far away green trees waving, and a flowing river that flashed in the sun, and rising above all, blue peaks of mountains.

"Oh, mother," he said; "untie the apron-string and let me go!"

But the mother said, "Not yet, my child! only yesterday you stumbled, and would have fallen but for the apron-string. Wait yet a little, till you are stronger."

So the boy waited, and all went as before; and the mother sang at her work.

But one day the boy found the door of the house standing open, for it was spring weather; and he stood on the threshold and looked across the valley, and saw the green trees waving, and the swift-flowing river with the sun flashing on it, and the blue mountains rising beyond; and this time he heard the voice of the river calling, and it said "Come!"

Then the boy started forward, and as he started, the string of the apron broke.

"Oh! how weak my mother's apron-string is!" cried the boy; and he ran out into the world, with the broken string hanging beside him.

The mother gathered up the other end of the string and put it in her bosom, and went about her work again; but she sang no more.

The boy ran on and on, rejoicing in his freedom, and in the fresh air and the morning sun. He crossed the valley, and began to climb the foothills among which the river flowed swiftly, among rocks and cliffs. Now it was easy climbing, and again it was steep and craggy, but always he looked upward at the blue peaks beyond, and always the voice of the river was in his ears, saying "Come!"

By and by he came to the brink of a precipice, over which the river dashed in a cataract, foaming and flashing, and sending up clouds of silver spray. The spray filled his eyes, so that he did not see his footing clearly; he grew dizzy, stumbled, and fell. But as he fell, something about him caught on a point of rock at the precipice-edge, and held him, so that he hung dangling over the abyss; and when he put up his hand to see what held him, he found that it was the broken string of the apron, which still hung by his side.

"Oh! how strong my mother's apron-string is!" said the boy: and he drew himself up by it, and stood firm on his feet, and went on climbing toward the blue peaks of the mountains.

THE SHADOW

N Angel heard a child crying one day, and came to see what ailed it. He found the little one sitting on the ground, with the sun at its back (for the day was young), looking at its own shadow, which lay on the ground before it, and weeping bitterly.

"What ails you, little one?" asked the Angel.

"The world is so dark!" said the child. "See, it is all dusky gray, and there is no beauty in it. Why must I stay in this sad, gray world?"

"Do you not hear the birds singing, and the other children calling at their play?" asked the Angel.

"Yes," said the child; "I hear them, but I do not know where they are. I cannot see them, I see only the shadow. Moreover, if they saw it, they would not sing and call, but would weep as I do."

The Angel lifted the child, and set it on its feet, with its face to the early sun.

"Look!" said the Angel.

The child brushed away the tears from its eyes and looked. Before them lay the fields all green and gold, shining with dewdrops, and the other children were running to and fro, laughing and shouting, and crowning one another with blossoms.

"Why, there are the children!" said the little one.

"Yes," said the Angel; "there they are."

"And the sun is shining!" cried the child.

"Yes," said the Angel; "it was shining all the time."

"And the shadow is gone!"

"Oh, no!" said the Angel; "the shadow is behind you, where it belongs. Run, now, and gather flowers for the littlest one, who sits in the grass there!"

THE SAILOR MAN

NCE upon a time two children came to the house of a sailor man, who lived beside the salt sea; and they found the sailor man sitting in his doorway knotting ropes.

"How do you do?" asked the sailor man.

"We are very well, thank you," said the children, who had learned manners, "and we hope you are the same. We heard that you had a boat, and we thought that perhaps you would take us out in her, and teach us how to sail, for that is what we wish most to know."

THE SAILOR MAN.

"All in good time," said the sailor man. "I am busy now, but by and by, when my work is done, I may perhaps take one of you if you are ready to learn. Meantime here are some ropes that need knotting; you might be doing that, since it has to be done." And he showed them how the knots should be tied, and went away and left them.

When he was gone the first child ran to the window and looked out.

"There is the sea," he said. "The waves come up on the beach, almost to the door of the house. They run up all white, like prancing horses, and then they go dragging back. Come and look!"

"I cannot," said the second child. "I am tying a knot."

"Oh!" cried the first child, "I see the boat. She is dancing like a lady at a ball; I never saw such a beauty. Come and look!"

"I cannot," said the second child. "I am tying a knot."

"I shall have a delightful sail in that boat," said the first child. "I expect that the sailor man will take me, because I am the eldest and I know more about it. There was no need of my watching when he showed you the knots, because I knew how already."

Just then the sailor man came in.

"Well," he said, "my work is over. What have you been doing in the meantime?"

"I have been looking at the boat," said the first child. "What a beauty she is! I shall have the best time in her that ever I had in my life."

"I have been tying knots," said the second child.

"Come, then," said the sailor man, and he held out his hand to the second child. "I will take you out in the boat, and teach you to sail her."

"But I am the eldest," cried the first child, "and I know a great deal more than she does."

"That may be," said the sailor man; "but a person must learn to tie a knot before he can learn to sail a boat."

"But I have learned to tie a knot," cried the child. "I know all about it!"

"How can I tell that?" asked the sailor man.

ITTLE boy," said the nurse one day, "you would be far better at work. Your garden needs weeding sadly; go now and weed it, like a good child!"
But the little boy did not feel like weeding that day.
"I can't do it," he said.
"Oh! yes, you can," said the nurse.
"Well, I don't want to," said the little boy.
"But you must!" said the nurse. "Don't be naughty, but go at once and do your work as I bid you!"
She went away about her own work, for she was very industrious; but the little boy sat still, and thought himself ill-used.
By and by his mother came into the room and saw him.

"What is the matter, little boy?" she asked; for he looked like a three-days' rain.
"Nurse told me to weed my garden," said the little boy.
"Oh," said his mother, "what fun that will be! I love to weed, and it is such a fine day! Mayn't I come and help?"
"Why, yes," said the little boy. "You may." And they weeded the garden beautifully, and had a glorious time.

NCE a child was sitting on a great log that lay by the roadside, playing; and another child came along, and stopped to speak to him.

"What are you doing?" asked the second child.

"I am sailing to the Southern Seas," replied the first, "to get a cargo of monkeys, and elephant tusks, and crystal balls as large as oranges. Come up here, and you may sail with me if you like."

So the second child climbed upon the log.

"Look!" said the first child. "See how the foam bubbles up before the ship, and trails and floats away behind! Look! the water is so clear that we can see the fishes swimming about, blue and red and green. There goes a parrot-fish; my father told me about them. I should not wonder if we saw a whale in about a minute."

"What are you talking about?" asked the second child, peevishly. "There is no water here, only grass; and anyhow this is nothing but a log. You cannot get to islands in this way."

"But we *have* got to them," cried the first child. "We are at them now. I see the palm-trees waving, and the white sand glittering. Look! there are the natives gathering to welcome us on the beach. They have feather cloaks, and necklaces, and anklets of copper as red as gold. Oh! and there is an elephant coming straight toward us."

"I should think you would be ashamed," said the second child. "That is Widow Slocum."

"It's all the same," said the first child.

Presently the second child got down from the log.

"I am going to play stick-knife," he said. "I don't see any sense in this. I think you are pretty dull to play things that aren't really there." And he walked slowly away.

The first child looked after him a moment.

"I think *you* are pretty dull," he said to himself, "to see nothing but what is under your nose."

But he was too well-mannered to say this aloud; and having taken in his cargo, he sailed for another port.

LITTLE JOHN BOTTLEJOHN

ITTLE John Bottlejohn lived on the hill,
And a blithe little man was he.
And he won the heart of a pretty mermaid
Who lived in the deep blue sea.
And every evening she used to sit
And sing on the rocks by the sea,
"Oh! little John Bottlejohn, pretty John Bottlejohn,
Won't you come out to me?"

Little John Bottlejohn heard her song,
And he opened his little door.
And he hopped and he skipped, and he skipped and he hopped,
Until he came down to the shore.
And there on the rocks sat the little mermaid,
And still she was singing so free,
"Oh! little John Bottlejohn, pretty John Bottlejohn,
Won't you come out to me?"

Little John Bottlejohn made a bow,
And the mermaid, she made one too,
And she said, "Oh! I never saw any one half
So perfectly sweet as you!
In my lovely home 'neath the ocean foam,
How happy we both might be!
Oh! little John Bottlejohn, pretty John Bottlejohn,
Won't you come down with me?"

Little John Bottlejohn said, "Oh yes!
I'll willingly go with you.
And I never shall quail at the sight of your tail,
For perhaps I may grow one too."
So he took her hand, and he left the land,
And plunged in the foaming main.
And little John Bottlejohn, pretty John Bottlejohn,
Never was seen again.

A FORTUNE

NE day a man was walking along the street, and he was sad at heart. Business was dull; he had set his desire upon a horse that cost a thousand dollars, and he had only eight hundred to buy it with. There were other things, to be sure, that might be bought with eight hundred dollars, but he did not want those; so he was sorrowful, and thought the world a bad place.

As he walked, he saw a child running toward him; it was a strange child, but when he looked at it, its face lightened like sunshine, and broke into smiles. The child held out its closed hand.

"Guess what I have!" it cried gleefully.

"Something fine, I am sure!" said the man.

The child nodded and drew nearer; then opened its hand.

"Look!" it said; and the street rang with its happy laughter. The man looked, and in the child's hand lay a penny.

"Hurrah!" said the child.

"Hurrah!" said the man.

Then they parted, and the child went and bought a stick of candy, and saw all the world red and white in stripes.

The man went and put his eight hundred dollars in the savings-bank, all but fifty cents, and with the fifty cents he bought a hobby-horse for his own little boy, and the little boy saw all the world brown, with white spots.

"Is this the horse you wanted so to buy, father?" asked the little boy.

"It is the horse I have bought!" said the man.

"Hurrah!" said the little boy.

"Hurrah!" said the man. And he saw that the world was a good place after all.

THE STARS

LITTLE dear child lay in its crib and sobbed, because it was afraid of the dark. And its father, in the room below, heard the sobs, and came up, and said, "What ails you, my dearie, and why do you cry?"

And the child said, "Oh, father, I am afraid of the dark. Nurse says I am too big to have a taper; but all the corners are full of dreadful blackness, and I think there are Things in them with eyes, that would look at me if I looked at them; and if they looked at me I should die. Oh, father, why is it dark? why is there such a terrible thing as darkness? why cannot it be always day?"

The father took the child in his arms and carried it downstairs and out into the summer night.

"Look up, dearie!" he said, in his strong, kind voice. "Look up, and see God's little lights!"

The little one looked up, and saw the stars, spangling the blue veil of the sky; bright as candles they burned, and yellow as gold.

"Oh, father," cried the child; "what are those lovely things?"

"Those are stars," said the father. "Those are God's little lights."

"But why have I never seen them before?"

"Because you are a very little child, and have never been out in the night before."

"Can I see the stars only at night, father?"

"Only at night, my child!"

"Do they only come then, father?"

"No; they are always there, but we cannot see them when the sun is shining."

"But, father, the darkness is not terrible here, it is beautiful!"

"Yes, dearie; the darkness is always beautiful, if we will only look up at the stars, instead of into the corners."

BUTTERCUP GOLD

H! the cupperty-buts! and oh! the cupperty-buts! out in the meadow, shining under the trees, and sparkling over the lawn, millions and millions of them, each one a bit of purest gold from Mother Nature's mint. Jessy stood at the window, looking out at them, and thinking, as she often had thought before, that there were no flowers so beautiful. "Cupperty-buts," she had been used to call them, when she was a wee baby-girl and could not speak without tumbling over her words and mixing them up in the queerest fashion; and now that she was a very great girl, actually six years old, they were still cupperty-buts to her, and would never be anything else,she said. There was nothing she liked better than to watch the lovely golden things, and nod to them as they nodded to her; but this morning her little face looked anxious and troubled, and she gazed at the flowers with an intent and inquiring look, as if she had expected them to reply to her unspoken thoughts. What these thoughts were I am going to tell you.

Half an hour before, she had called to her mother, who was just going out, and begged her to come and look at the cupperty-buts.

"They are brighter than ever, Mamma! Do just come and look at them! golden, golden, golden! There must be fifteen thousand million dollars' worth of gold just on the lawn, I should think."

And her mother, pausing to look out, said, very sadly,—

"Ah, my darling! if I only had this day a little of that gold, what a happy woman I should be!"

And then the good mother went out, and there little Jessy stood, gazing at the flowers, and repeating the words to herself, over and over again,—

"If I only had a little of that gold!"

She knew that her mother was very, very poor, and had to go out to work every day to earn food and clothes for herself and her little daughter; and the child's tender heart ached to think of the sadness in the dear mother's look and tone. Suddenly Jessy started, and the sunshine flashed into her face.

"Why!" she exclaimed, "why shouldn't I get some of the gold from the cupperty-buts? I believe I could get some, perfectly well. When Mamma wants to get the juice out of anything, meat, or fruit, or anything of that sort, she just boils it. And so, if I should boil the cupperty-buts, wouldn't all the gold come out? Of course it would! Oh, joy! how pleased Mamma will be!"

Jessy's actions always followed her thoughts with great rapidity. In five minutes she was out on the lawn, with a huge basket beside her, pulling away at the buttercups with might and main. Oh! how small they were, and how long it took even to cover the bottom of the basket. But Jessy worked with a will, and at the end of an hour she had picked enough to make at least a thousand dollars, as she calculated. That would do for one day, she thought; and now for the grand experiment! Before going out she had with much labor filled the great kettle with water, so now the water was boiling, and she had only to put the buttercups in and put the cover on. When this was done, she sat as patiently as she could, trying to pay attention to her knitting, and not to look at the clock oftener than every two minutes.

"They must boil for an hour," she said; "and by that time all the gold will have come out."

Well, the hour did pass, somehow or other, though it was a very long one; and at eleven o'clock, Jessy, with a mighty effort, lifted the kettle from the stove and carried it to the open door, that the fresh air might cool the boiling water. At first, when she lifted the cover, such a cloud of steam came out that she could see nothing; but in a moment the wind blew the steam aside, and then she saw,—oh, poor little Jessy!—she saw a mass ofweeds floating about in a quantity of dirty, greenish water, and that was all. Not the smallest trace of gold, even in the buttercups themselves, was to be seen. Poor little Jessy! she tried hard not to cry, but it was a bitter disappointment; the tears came rolling down her cheeks faster and faster, till at length she sat down by the kettle, and, burying her face in her apron, sobbed as if her heart would break.

Presently, through her sobs, she heard a kind voice saying, "What is the matter, little one? Why do you cry so bitterly?" She looked up and saw an old gentleman with white hair and a bright, cheery face, standing by her. At first, Jessy could say nothing but "Oh! the cupperty-buts! oh! the cupperty-buts!" but, of course, the old gentleman didn't know what she meant by that, so, as he urged her to tell him about her trouble, she dried her eyes, and told him the melancholy little story: how her mother was very poor, and said she wished she had some gold; and how she herself had tried to get the gold out of the buttercups by boiling them. "I was so sure I could get it out," she said, "and I thought Mamma would be so pleased! And now—"

Here she was very near breaking down again; but the gentleman patted her head and said, cheerfully, "Wait a bit, little woman! Don't give up the ship yet. You know that gold is heavy, very heavy indeed, and if there were any it would be at the very bottom of the kettle, all covered with the weeds, so that you could not see it. I should not be at all surprised if you found some, after all.

Run into the house and bring me a spoon with a long handle, and we will fish in the kettle, and see what we can find."

Jessy's face brightened, and she ran into the house. If any one had been standing near just at that moment, I think it is possible that he might have seen the old gentleman's hand go into his pocket and out again very quickly, and might have heard a little splash in the kettle; but nobody was near, so, of course, I cannot say anything about it. At any rate, when Jessy came out with the spoon, he was standing with both hands in his pockets, looking in the opposite direction. He took the great iron spoon and fished about in the kettle for some time. At last there was a little clinking noise, and the old gentleman lifted the spoon. Oh, wonder and delight! In it lay three great, broad, shining pieces of gold! Jessy could hardly believe her eyes. She stared and stared; and when the old gentleman put the gold into her hand, she still stood as if in a happy dream, gazing at it. Suddenly she started, and remembered that she had not thanked her kindly helper. She looked up, and began, "Thank you, sir;" but the old gentleman was gone.

Well, the next question was, How could Jessy possibly wait till twelve o'clock for her mother to come home? Knitting was out of the question. She could do nothing but dance and look out of window, and look out of window and dance, holding the precious coins tight in her hand. At last, a well-known footstep was heard outside the door, and Mrs. Gray came in, looking very tired and worn. She smiled, however, when she saw Jessy, and said,—

"Well, my darling, I am glad to see you looking so bright. How has the morning gone with my little housekeeper?"

"Oh, mother!" cried Jessy, hopping about on one foot, "it has gone very well! oh, very, *very, very* well! Oh, my mother dear, what do you think I have got in my hand? *What* do you think? oh, what *do* you think?" and she went dancing round and round, till poor Mrs. Gray was quite dizzy with watching her. At last she stopped, and holding out her hand, opened it and showed her mother what was in it. Mrs. Gray was really frightened.

"Jessy, my child!" she cried, "where did you get all that money?"

"Out of the cupperty-buts, Mamma!" said Jessy, "out of the cupperty-buts! and it's all for you, every bit of it! Dear Mamma, now you will be happy, will you not?"

"Jessy," said Mrs. Gray, "have you lost your senses, or are you playing some trick on me? Tell me all about this at once, dear child, and don't talk nonsense."

"But it isn't nonsense, Mamma!" cried Jessy, "and it did come out of the cupperty-buts!"

And then she told her mother the whole story. The tears came into Mrs. Gray's eyes, but they were tears of joy and gratitude.

"Jessy dear," she said, "when we say our prayers at night, let us never forget to pray for that good gentleman. May Heaven bless him and reward him! for if it had not been for him, Jessy dear, I fear you would never have found the 'Buttercup Gold.'"

THE PATIENT CAT

HEN the spotted cat first found the nest, there was nothing in it, for it was only just finished. So she said, "I will wait!" for she was a patient cat, and the summer was before her. She waited a week, and then she climbed up again to the top of the tree, and peeped into the nest. There lay two lovely blue eggs, smooth and shining.

The spotted cat said, "Eggs may be good, but young birds are better. I will wait." So she waited; and while she was waiting, she caught mice and rats, and washed herself and slept, and did all that a spotted cat should do to pass the time away.

When another week had passed, she climbed the tree again and peeped into the nest. This time there were five eggs. But the spotted cat said again, "Eggs may be good, but young birds are better. I will wait a little longer!"

So she waited a little longer and then went up again to look. Ah! there were five tiny birds, with big eyes and long necks, and yellow beaks wide open. Then the spotted cat sat down on the branch, and licked her nose and purred, for she was very happy. "It is worth while to be patient!" she said.

But when she looked again at the young birds, to see which one she should take first, she saw that they were very thin,—oh, very, very thin they were! The spotted cat had never seen anything so thin in her life.

"Now," she said to herself, "if I were to wait only a few days longer, they would grow fat. Thin birds may be good, but fat birds are much better. I will wait!"

So she waited; and she watched the father-bird bringing worms all day long to the nest, and said, "Aha! they must be fattening fast! they will soon be as fat as I wish them to be. Aha! what a good thing it is to be patient."

At last, one day she thought, "Surely, now they must be fat enough! I will not wait another day. Aha! how good they will be!"

So she climbed up the tree, licking her chops all the way and thinking of the fat young birds. And when she reached the top and looked into the nest, it was empty!!

Then the spotted cat sat down on the branch and spoke thus, "Well, of all the horrid, mean, ungrateful creatures I ever saw, those birds are the horridest, and the meanest, and the most ungrateful! Mi-a-u-ow!!!!"

ALICE'S SUPPER

AR down in the meadow the wheat grows green,
And the reapers are whetting their sickles so keen;
And this is the song that I hear them sing,
While cheery and loud their voices ring:
"'Tis the finest wheat that ever did grow!
And it is for Alice's supper, ho! ho!"

Far down in the valley the old mill stands,
And the miller is rubbing his dusty white hands;
And these are the words of the miller's lay,
As he watches the millstones a-grinding away:
"'Tis the finest flour that money can buy,
And it is for Alice's supper, hi! hi!"

Downstairs in the kitchen the fire doth glow,
And Maggie is kneading the soft white dough,
And this is the song that she's singing to-day,
While merry and busy she's working away:
"'Tis the finest dough, by near or by far,
And it is for Alice's supper, ha! ha!"

And now to the nursery comes Nannie at last,
And what in her hand is she bringing so fast?
'Tis a plate full of something all yellow and white,
And she sings as she comes with her smile so bright:
"'Tis the best bread-and-butter I ever did see!
And it is for Alice's supper, he! he!"

THE QUACKY DUCK

HE Quacky Duck stood on the bank of the stream. And the frogs came and sat on stones and insulted him. Now the words which the frogs used were these,—
"Ya! ha! he hasn't any hind-legs!Ya! ha! he hasn't any fore-legs!Oh! what horrid luckTo be a Quacky Duck!"

These were not pleasant words. And when the Quacky Duck heard them, he considered within himself whether it would not be best for him to eat the frogs.

"Two good things would come of it," he said. "I should have a savoury meal, and their remarks would no longer be audible."

So he fell upon the frogs, and they fled before him. And one jumped into the water, and one jumped on the land, and another jumped into the reeds; for such is their manner. But one of them, being in fear, saw not clearly the way he should go, and jumped even upon the back of the Quacky Duck. Now, this displeased the Quacky Duck, and he said, "If you will remove yourself from my person, we will speak further of this."

So the frog, being also willing, strove to remove himself, and the result was that they two, being on the edge of the bank, fell into the water. Then the frog departed swiftly, saying, "Solitude is best for meditation."

But the Quacky Duck, having hit his head against a stone, sank to the bottom of the pond, where he found himself in the frogs' kitchen. And there he spied a fish, which the frogs had caught for their dinner, intending to share it in a brotherly manner, for it was a savoury fish. When the Quacky Duck saw it, he was glad; and he said, "Fish is better than frog" (for he was an English duck)! And, taking the fish, he swam with speed to the shore.

Now the frogs lamented when they saw him go, for they said, "He has our savoury fish!" And they wept, and reviled the Quacky Duck.

But he said, "Be comforted! for if I had not found the fish, I should assuredly have eaten you. Therefore, say now, which is the better for you?" And he ate the fish, and departed joyful.

AT THE LITTLE BOY'S HOME

T was a very hot day, and the little boy was lying on his stomach under the big linden tree, reading the "Scottish Chiefs."

"Little Boy," said his mother, "will you please go out in the garden and bring me a head of lettuce?"

"Oh, I—can't!" said the little boy. "I'm—too—*hot!*"

The little boy's father happened to be close by, weeding the geranium bed; and when he heard this, he lifted the little boy gently by his waistband, and dipped him in the great tub of water that stood ready for watering the plants.

"There, my son!" said the father. "Now you are cool enough to go and get the lettuce; but remember next time that it will be easier to go at once when you are told, as then you will not have to change your clothes."

The little boy went drip, drip, dripping out into the garden and brought the lettuce; then he went drip, drip, dripping into the house and changed his clothes; but he said never a word, for he knew there was nothing to say.

That is the way they do things where the little boy lives. Would you like to live there? Perhaps not; yet he is a happy little boy, and he is learning the truth of the old saying,—

"Come when you're called, do as you're bid,Shut the door after you, and you'll never be chid."

NEW YEAR

HE little sweet Child tied on her hood, and put on her warm cloak and mittens. "I am going to the wood," she said, "to tell the creatures all about it. They cannot understand about Christmas, mamma says, and of course she knows, but I do think they ought to know about New Year!"

Out in the wood the snow lay light and powdery on the branches, but under foot it made a firm, smooth floor, over which the Child could walk lightly without sinking in. She saw other footprints beside her own, tiny bird-tracks, little hopping marks, which showed where a rabbit had taken his way, traces of mice and squirrels and other little wild-wood beasts.

The child stood under a great hemlock-tree, and looked up toward the clear blue sky, which shone far away beyond the dark tree-tops. She spread her hands abroad and called, "Happy New Year! Happy New Year to everybody in the wood, and all over the world!"

A rustling was heard in the hemlock branches, and a striped squirrel peeped down at her. "What do you mean by that, little Child?" he asked. And then from all around came other squirrels, came little field-mice, and hares swiftly leaping, and all the winter birds, titmouse and snow-bird, and many another; and they all wanted to know what the Child meant by her greeting, for they had never heard the words before.

"It means that God is giving us another year!" said the Child. "Four more seasons, each lovelier than the last, just as it was last year. Flowers will bud, and then they will blossom, and then the fruit will hang all red and golden on the branches, for birds and men and little children to eat." "And squirrels, too!" cried the chipmunk, eagerly.

"Of course!" said the Child. "Squirrels, too, and every creature that lives in the good green wood. And this is not all! We can do over again the things that we tried to do last year, and perhaps failed in doing. We have another chance to be good and kind, to do little loving things that help, and to cure ourselves of doing naughty things. Our hearts can have lovely new seasons, like the flowers and trees and all the sweet things that grow and bear leaves and fruit. I thought I would come and tell you all this, because sometimes one does not think of things till one hears them from another's lips. Are you glad I came? If you are glad, say Happy New Year! each in his own way! I say it to you all now in my way. Happy New Year! Happy New Year!"

Such a noise as broke out then had never been heard in the wood since the oldest hemlock was a baby, and that was a long time ago. Chirping, twittering, squeaking, chattering! The wood-doves lit on the Child's shoulder and cooed in her ear, and she knew just what they said. The squirrels made a long speech, and meant every word of it, which is more than people always do; the field-mouse said that she was going to turn over a new leaf, the very biggest cabbage-leaf she could find; while the titmouse invited the whole company to dine with him, a thing he had never done in his life before.

When the Child turned to leave the wood, the joyful chorus followed her, and she went, smiling, home and told her mother all about it. "And, mother," she said, "I should not be surprised if they had got a little bit of Christmas, after all, along with their New Year!"

JACKY FROST

ACKY Frost, Jacky Frost,
Came in the night;
Left the meadows that he crossed
All gleaming white.
Painted with his silver brush
Every window-pane;
Kissed the leaves and made them blush,
Blush and blush again.

Jacky Frost, Jacky Frost,
Crept around the house,
Sly as a silver fox,
Still as a mouse.
Out little Jenny came,
Blushing like a rose;
Up jumped Jacky Frost,
And pinched her little nose.

NCE a Cake would go seek his fortune in the world, and he took his leave of the Pan he was baked in.

"I know my destiny," said the Cake. "I must be eaten, since to that end I was made; but I am a good cake, if I say it who should not, and I would fain choose the persons I am to benefit."

"I don't see what difference it makes to you!" said the Pan.

"But imagination is hardly your strong point!" said the Cake.

"Huh!" said the Pan.

The Cake went on his way, and soon he passed by a cottage door where sat a woman spinning, and her ten children playing about her.

"Oh!" said the woman, "what a beautiful cake!" and she put out her hand to take him.

"Be so good as to wait a moment!" said the Cake. "Will you kindly tell me what you would do with me if I should yield myself up to you?"

"I shall break you into ten pieces," said the woman, "and give one to each of my ten children. So you will give ten pleasures, and that is a good thing."

"Oh, that would be very nice, I am sure," said the Cake; "but if you will excuse me for mentioning it, your children seem rather dirty, especially their hands, and I confess I should like to keep my frosting unsullied, so I think I will go a little further."

"As you will!" said the woman. "After all, the brown loaf is better for the children."

So the Cake went further, and met a fair child, richly dressed, with coral lips and eyes like sunlit water. When the child saw the Cake, he said like the woman, "Oh, what a beautiful Cake!" and put out his hand to take it.

"I am sure I should be most happy!" said the Cake. "And you will not take it amiss, I am confident, if I ask with whom you will share me."

"I shall not share you with any one!" said the child. "I shall eat you myself, every crumb. What do you take me for?"

"Good gracious!" cried the Cake. "This will never do. Consider my size,—and yours! You would be very ill!"

"I don't care!" said the child. "I'd rather be ill than give any away." And he fixed greedy eyes on the Cake, and stretched forth his hand again.

"This is really terrible!" cried the Cake. "What is one's frosting to this? I will go back to the woman with the ten children."

He turned and ran back, leaving the child screaming with rage and disappointed greed. But as he ran, a hungry Puppy met him, and swallowed him at a gulp, and went on licking his chops and wagging his tail.

"Huh!" said the Pan.

HIMBORAZO was a very unhappy boy. He pouted, and he sulked, and he said, "Oh, dear! oh, dear! oh, dear! oh, dear!" He said it till everybody was tired of hearing it.

"Chimborazo," his mother would say, "please don't say, 'Oh, dear!' any more. It is very annoying. Say something else."

"Oh, dear!" the boy would answer, "I can't! I don't know anything else to say. Oh, dear! Oh, *dear*!! oh, DEAR!!!"

One day his mother could not bear it any longer, and she sent for his fairy godmother, and told her all about it.

"Humph!" said the fairy godmother. "I will see to it. Send the boy to me!"

So Chimborazo was sent for, and came, hanging his head as usual. When he saw his fairy godmother, he said, "Oh, dear!" for he was rather afraid of her.

"'Oh, dear!' it is!" said the godmother sharply; and she put on her spectacles and looked at him. "Do you know what a bell-punch is?"

"Oh, dear!" said Chimborazo. "No, ma'am, I don't!"

"Well," said the godmother, "I am going to give you one."

"Oh, dear!" said Chimborazo, "I don't want one."

"Probably not," replied she, "but that doesn't make much difference. You have it now, in your jacket pocket."

Chimborazo felt in his pocket, and took out a queer-looking instrument of shining metal. "Oh, dear!" he said.

"'Oh, dear!' it is!" said the fairy godmother. "Now," she continued, "listen to me, Chimborazo! I am going to put you on an allowance of 'Oh, dears.' This is a self-acting bell-punch, and it will ring whenever you say 'Oh, dear!' How many times do you generally say it in the course of the day?"

"Oh, dear!" said Chimborazo, "I don't know. Oh, *dear*!"

"*Ting! ting!*" the bell-punch rang twice sharply; and looking at it in dismay, he saw two little round holes punched in a long slip of pasteboard which was fastened to the instrument.

"Exactly!" said the fairy. "That is the way it works, and a very pretty way, too. Now, my boy, I am going to make you a very liberal allowance. You may say 'Oh, dear!' forty-five times a day. There's liberality for you!"

"Oh, dear!" cried Chimborazo, "I——"

"*Ting!*" said the bell-punch.

"You see!" observed the fairy. "Nothing could be prettier. You have now had three of this day's allowance. It is still some hours before noon, so I advise you to be careful. If you exceed the allowance——" Here she paused, and glowered through her spectacles in a very dreadful manner.

"Oh, dear!" cried Chimborazo. "What will happen then?"

"You will see!" said the fairy godmother, with a nod. "*Something* will happen, you may be very sure of that. Good-by. Remember, only forty-five!" And away she flew out of the window.

"Oh, dear!" cried Chimborazo, bursting into tears. "I don't want it! I won't have it! Oh, *dear!* oh, dear! oh, dear! oh, dear! oh, DEAR!!!"

"Ting! ting! ting-ting-ting-*ting!*" said the bell-punch; and now there were ten round holes in the strip of pasteboard. Chimborazo was now really frightened. He was silent for some time; and when his mother called him to his lessons he tried very hard not to say the dangerous words. But the habit was so strong that he said them unconsciously. By dinnertime there were twenty-five holes in the cardboard strip; by tea-time there were forty! Poor Chimborazo! he was afraid to open his lips, for whenever he did the words would slip out in spite of him.

"Well, Chimbo," said his father after tea, "I hear you have had a visit from your fairy godmother. What did she say to you, eh?"

"Oh, dear!" said Chimborazo, "she said—oh, dear! I've said it again!"

"She said, 'Oh, dear! I've said it again!'" repeated his father. "What do you mean by that?"

"Oh, dear! I didn't mean that," cried Chimborazo hastily; and again the inexorable bell rang, and he knew that another hole was punched in the fatal cardboard. He pressed his lips firmly together, and did not open them again except to say "Good-night," until he was safe in his own room. Then he hastily drew the hated bell-punch from his pocket, and counted the holes in the strip of cardboard; there were forty-three! "Oh, *dear!*" cried the boy, forgetting himself again in his alarm, "only two more! Oh, *dear!* oh, DEAR! I've done it again! oh——" "Ting! ting!" went the bell-punch; and the cardboard was punched to the end. "Oh, dear!" cried Chimborazo, now beside himself with terror. "Oh, dear! oh, dear! oh, dear! oh, *dear!!* what will become of me?"

A strange whirring noise was heard, then a loud clang; and the next moment the bell-punch, as if it were alive, flew out of his hand, out of the window, and was gone!

Chimborazo stood breathless with terror for a few minutes, momentarily expecting that the roof would fall in on his head, or the floor blow up under his feet, or some appalling catastrophe of some kind follow; but nothing followed. Everything was quiet, and there seemed to be nothing to do but go to bed; and so to bed he went, and slept, only to dream that he was shot through the head with a bell-punch, and died saying, "Oh, dear!"

The next morning, when Chimborazo came downstairs, his father said, "My boy, I am going to drive over to your grandfather's farm this morning; would you like to go with me?"

A drive to the farm was one of the greatest pleasures Chimborazo had, so he answered promptly, "Oh, *dear!*"

"Oh, very well!" said his father, looking much surprised. "You need not go, my son, if you do not want to. I will take Robert instead."

Poor Chimborazo! He had opened his lips to say, "Thank you, papa. I should like to go *very* much!" and, instead of these words, out had popped, in his most doleful tone, the now hated "Oh, dear!" He sat amazed; but was roused by his mother's calling him to breakfast.

"Come, Chimbo," she said. "Here are sausages and scrambled eggs: and you are very fond of both of them. Which will you have?"

Chimborazo hastened to say, "Sausages, please, mamma,"—that is, he hastened to *try* to say it; but all his mother heard was, "Oh, *dear!*"

His father looked much displeased. "Give the boy some bread and water, wife," he said sternly. "If he cannot answer properly, he must be taught. I have had enough of this 'oh, dear!' business."

Poor Chimborazo! He saw plainly enough now what his punishment was to be; and the thought of it made him tremble. He tried to ask for some more bread, but only brought out his "Oh, *dear!*" in such a lamentable tone that his father ordered him to leave the room. He went out into the garden, and there he met John the gardener, carrying a basket of rosy apples. Oh! how good they looked!

"I am bringing some of the finest apples up to the house, little master," said John. "Will you have one to put in your pocket?"

"Oh, *dear!*" was all the poor boy could say, though he wanted an apple, oh, so much! And when John heard that he put the apple back in his basket, muttering something about ungrateful monkeys.

Poor Chimborazo! I will not give the whole history of that miserable day,—a miserable day it was from beginning to end. He fared no better at dinner than at breakfast; for at the second "Oh, dear!" his father sent him up to his room, "to stay there until he knew how to take what was given him, and be thankful for it." He knew well enough by this time; but he could not tell his father so. He went to his room, and sat looking out of the window, a hungry and miserable boy.

In the afternoon his cousin Will came up to see him. "Why, Chimbo!" he cried. "Why do you sit moping here in the house, when all the boys are out? Come and play marbles with me on the piazza. Ned and Harry are out there waiting for you. Come on!"

"Oh, dear!" said Chimborazo.

"What's the matter?" asked Will. "Haven't you any marbles? Never mind. I'll give you half of mine, if you like. Come!"

"Oh, DEAR!" said Chimborazo.

"Well," said Will, "if that's all you have to say when I offer you marbles, I'll keep them myself. I suppose you expected me to give you all of them, did you? I never saw such a fellow!" and off he went in a huff.

"Well, Chimborazo," said the fairy godmother, "what do you think of 'Oh, dear!' now?"

Chimborazo looked at her beseechingly, but said nothing.

"Finding that forty-five times was not enough for you yesterday, I thought I would let you have all you wanted to-day, you see," said the fairy wickedly.

The boy still looked imploringly at her, but did not open his lips.

"Well, well," she said at last, touching his lips with her wand, "I think that is enough in the way of punishment, though I am sorry you broke the bell-punch. Good-by! I don't believe you will say 'Oh, dear!' any more."

And he didn't.

THE USEFUL COAL

HERE was once a king whose name was Sligo. He was noted both for his riches and his kind heart. One evening, as he sat by his fireside, a coal fell out on the hearth. The king took up the tongs, intending to put it back on the fire, but the coal said:—

"If you will spare my life, and do as I tell you, I will save your treasure three times, and tell you the name of the thief who steals it."

These words gave the king great joy, for much treasure had been stolen from him of late, and none of his officers could discover the culprit. So he set the coal on the table, and said:—

"Pretty little black and red bird, tell me, what shall I do?"

"Put me in your waistcoat-pocket," said the coal, "and take no more thought for to-night."

Accordingly the king put the coal in his pocket, and then, as he sat before the warm fire, he grew drowsy, and presently fell fast asleep.

When he had been asleep some time, the door opened, very softly, and the High Cellarer peeped cautiously in. This was the one of the king's officers who had been most eager in searching for the thief. He now crept softly, softly, toward the king, and seeing that he was fast asleep, put his hand into his waistcoat-pocket; for in that waistcoat-pocket King Sligo kept the key of his treasure-chamber, and the High Cellarer was the thief. He put his hand into the waistcoat-pocket. S-s-s-s-s! the coal burned it so frightfully that he gave a loud shriek, and fell on his knees on the hearth.

"What is the matter?" cried the king, waking with a start.

"Alas! your Majesty," said the High Cellarer, thrusting his burnt fingers into his bosom, that the king might not see them. "You were just on the point of falling forward into the fire, and I cried out, partly from fright and partly to waken you."

The king thanked the High Cellarer, and gave him a ruby ring as a reward. But when he was in his chamber, and making ready for bed, the coal said to him:—

"Once already have I saved your treasure, and to-night I shall save it again. Only put me on the table beside your bed, and you may sleep with a quiet heart."

So the king put the coal on the table, and himself into the bed, and was soon sound asleep. At midnight the door of the chamber opened very softly, and the High Cellarer peeped in again. He knew that at night King Sligo kept the key under his pillow, and he was coming to get it. He crept softly, softly, toward the bed, but as he drew near it, the coal cried out:—

"One eye sleeps, but the other eye wakes! one eye sleeps, but the other eye wakes! Who is this comes creeping, while honest men are sleeping?"

The High Cellarer looked about him in affright, and saw the coal burning fiery red in the darkness, and looking for all the world like a great flaming eye. In an agony of fear he fled from the chamber, crying,—

"Black and red! black and red!The king has a devil to guard his bed."

And he spent the rest of the night shivering in the farthest garret he could find.

The next morning the coal said to the king:—

"Again this night have I saved your treasure, and mayhap your life as well. Yet a third time I shall do it, and this time you shall learn the name of the thief. But if I do this, you must promise me one thing, and that is that you will place me in your royal crown and wear me as a jewel. Will you do this?"

"That will I, right gladly!" replied King Sligo, "for a jewel indeed you are."

"That is well!" said the coal. "It is true that I am dying; but no matter. It is a fine thing to be a jewel in a king's crown, even if one is dead. Now listen, and follow my directions closely. As soon as I am quite black and dead,—which will be in about ten minutes from now,—you must take me in your hand and rub me all over and around the handle of the door of the treasure-chamber. A good part of me will be rubbed off, but there will be enough left to put in your crown. When you have thoroughly rubbed the door, lay the key of the treasure-chamber on your table, as if you had left it there by mistake. You may then go hunting or riding, but not for more than an hour; and when you return, you must instantly call all your court together, as if on business of the greatest importance. Invent some excuse for asking them to raise their hands, and then arrest the man whose hands are black. Do you understand?"

"I do!" replied King Sligo, fervently, "I do, and my warmest thanks, good Coal, are due to you for this—"

But here he stopped, for already the coal was quite black, and in less than ten minutes it was dead and cold. Then the king took it and rubbed it carefully over the door of the treasure-chamber, and laying the key of the door in plain sight on his dressing-table, he called his huntsmen together, and mounting his horse, rode away to the forest. As soon as he was gone, the High Cellarer, who had pleaded a headache when asked to join the hunt, crept softly to the king's room, and to his surprise found the key on the table. Full of joy, he sought the treasure-chamber at once, and began filling his pockets with gold and jewels, which he carried to his own apartment, returning greedily for more. In this way he opened and closed the door many times. Suddenly, as he was stooping over

a silver barrel containing sapphires, he heard the sound of a trumpet, blown
once, twice, thrice. The wicked thief started, for it was the signal for the entire
court to appear instantly before the king, and the penalty of disobedience was
death. Hastily cramming a handful of sapphires into his pocket, he stumbled to
the door, which he closed and locked, putting the key also in his pocket, as
there was no time to return it. He flew to the presence-chamber, where the
lords of the kingdom were hastily assembling.

The king was seated on his throne, still in his hunting-dress, though he had
put on his crown over his hat, which presented a peculiar appearance. It was
with a majestic air, however, that he rose and said:—

"Nobles, and gentlemen of my court! I have called you together to pray for the
soul of my lamented grandmother, who died, as you may remember, several
years ago. In token of respect, I desire you all to raise your hands to Heaven."

The astonished courtiers, one and all, lifted their hands high in air. The king
looked, and, behold! the hands of the High Cellarer were as black as soot! The
king caused him to be arrested and searched, and the sapphires in his pocket,
besides the key of the treasure-chamber, gave ample proof of his guilt. His
head was removed at once, and the king had the useful coal, set in sapphires,
placed in the very front of his crown, where it was much admired and praised
as a BLACK DIAMOND.

SONG OF THE LITTLE WINDS

THE birdies may sleep, but the winds must wake
Early and late, for the birdies' sake.
Kissing them, fanning them, soft and sweet,
E'en till the dark and the dawning meet.

The flowers may sleep, but the winds must wake
Early and late, for the flowers' sake.
Rocking the buds on the rose-mother's breast,
Swinging the hyacinth-bells to rest.

The children may sleep, but the winds must wake
Early and late, for the children's sake.
Singing so sweet in each little one's ear,
He thinks his mother's own song to hear.

THE THREE REMARKS

THERE was once a princess, the most beautiful princess that ever was seen. Her hair was black and soft as the raven's wing; her eyes were like stars dropped in a pool of clear water, and her speech like the first tinkling cascade of the baby Nile. She was also wise, graceful, and gentle, so that one would have thought she must be the happiest princess in the world.

But, alas! there was one terrible drawback to her happiness. She could make only three remarks. No one knew whether it was the fault of her nurse, or a peculiarity born with her; but the sad fact remained, that no matter what was said to her, she could only reply in one of three phrases. The first was,—

"What is the price of butter?"
The second, "Has your grandmother sold her mangle yet?"
And the third, "With all my heart!"
You may well imagine what a great misfortune this was to a young and lively princess. How could she join in the sports and dances of the noble youths and maidens of the court? She could not always be silent, neither could she always say, "With all my heart!" though this was her favorite phrase, and she used it whenever she possibly could; and it was not at all pleasant, when some gallant

knight asked her whether she would rather play croquet or Aunt Sally, to be obliged to reply, "What is the price of butter?"

On certain occasions, however, the princess actually found her infirmity of service to her. She could always put an end suddenly to any conversation that did not please her, by interposing with her first or second remark; and they were also a very great assistance to her when, as happened nearly every day, she received an offer of marriage. Emperors, kings, princes, dukes, earls, marquises, viscounts, baronets, and many other lofty personages knelt at her feet, and offered her their hands, hearts, and other possessions of greater or less value. But for all her suitors the princess had but one answer. Fixing her deep radiant eyes on them, she would reply with thrilling earnestness, "*Has* your grandmother sold her mangle yet?" and this always impressed the suitors so deeply that they retired, weeping, to a neighboring monastery, where they hung up their armor in the chapel, and taking the vows, passed the remainder of their lives mostly in flogging themselves, wearing hair shirts, and putting dry toast-crumbs in their beds.

Now, when the king found that all his best nobles were turning into monks, he was greatly displeased, and said to the princess:—

"My daughter, it is high time that all this nonsense came to an end. The next time a respectable person asks you to marry him, you will say, 'With all my heart!' or I will know the reason why."

But this the princess could not endure, for she had never yet seen a man whom she was willing to marry. Nevertheless, she feared her father's anger, for she knew that he always kept his word; so that very night she slipped down the back stairs of the palace, opened the back door, and ran away out into the wide world.

She wandered for many days, over mountain and moor, through fen and through forest, until she came to a fair city. Here all the bells were ringing, and the people shouting and flinging caps into the air; for their old king was dead, and they were just about to crown a new one. The new king was a stranger, who had come to the town only the day before; but as soon as he heard of the old monarch's death, he told the people that he was a king himself, and as he happened to be without a kingdom at that moment, he would be quite willing to rule over them. The people joyfully assented, for the late king had left no heir; and now all the preparations had been completed. The crown had been polished up, and a new tip put on the sceptre, as the old king had quite spoiled it by poking the fire with it for upwards of forty years.

When the people saw the beautiful princess, they welcomed her with many bows, and insisted on leading her before the new king.

"Who knows but that they may be related?" said everybody. "They both came from the same direction, and both are strangers."

Accordingly the princess was led to the market-place, where the king was sitting in royal state. He had a fat, red, shining face, and did not look like the kings whom she had been in the habit of seeing; but nevertheless the princess made a graceful courtesy, and then waited to hear what he would say.

The new king seemed rather embarrassed when he saw that it was a princess who appeared before him; but he smiled graciously, and said, in a smooth oily voice,—

"I trust your 'Ighness is quite well. And 'ow did yer 'Ighness leave yer pa and ma?"

At these words the princess raised her head and looked fixedly at the red-faced king; then she replied, with scornful distinctness,—

"What is the price of butter?"

At these words an alarming change came over the king's face. The red faded from it, and left it a livid green; his teeth chattered; his eyes stared, and rolled in their sockets; while the sceptre dropped from his trembling hand and fell at the princess's feet. For the truth was, this was no king at all, but a retired butterman, who had laid by a little money at his trade, and had thought of setting up a public house; but chancing to pass through this city at the very time when they were looking for a king, it struck him that he might just as well fill the vacant place as any one else. No one had thought of his being an impostor; but when the princess fixed her clear eyes on him and asked him that familiar question, which he had been in the habit of hearing many times a day for a great part of his life, the guilty butterman thought himself detected, and shook in his guilty shoes. Hastily descending from his throne, he beckoned the princess into a side-chamber, and closing the door, besought her in moving terms not to betray him.

"Here," he said, "is a bag of rubies as big as pigeon's eggs. There are six thousand of them, and I 'umbly beg your 'Ighness to haccept them as a slight token hof my hesteem, if your 'Ighness will kindly consent to spare a respeckable tradesman the disgrace of being hexposed."

The princess reflected, and came to the conclusion that, after all, a butterman might make as good a king as any one else; so she took the rubies with a gracious little nod, and departed, while all the people shouted, "Hooray!" and followed her, waving their hats and kerchiefs, to the gates of the city.

With her bag of rubies over her shoulder, the fair princess now pursued her journey, and fared forward over heath and hill, through brake and through brier. After several days she came to a deep forest, which she entered without hesitation, for she knew no fear. She had not gone a hundred paces under the arching limes, when she was met by a band of robbers, who stopped her and asked what she did in their forest, and what she carried in her bag. They were fierce, black-bearded men, armed to the teeth with daggers, cutlasses, pistols, dirks, hangers, blunderbusses, and other defensive weapons; but the princess gazed calmly on them, and said haughtily,—

"Has your grandmother sold her mangle yet?"

The effect was magical. The robbers started back in dismay, crying, "The countersign!" Then they hastily lowered their weapons, and assuming attitudes of abject humility, besought the princess graciously to accompany them to their master's presence. With a lofty gesture she signified assent, and the cringing, trembling bandits led her on through the forest till they reached an open glade, into which the sunbeams glanced right merrily. Here, under a broad oak-tree which stood in the centre of the glade, reclined a man of gigantic stature and commanding mien, with a whole armory of weapons displayed upon his person. Hastening to their chief, the robbers conveyed to him, in agitated whispers, the circumstance of their meeting the princess, and of her unexpected reply to their questions. Hardly seeming to credit their statement, the gigantic chieftain sprang to his feet, and advancing toward the princess with a respectful reverence, begged her to repeat the remark which had so disturbed his men. With a royal air, and in clear and ringing tones, the princess repeated,—

"*Has* your grandmother sold her mangle yet?" and gazed steadfastly at the robber chief.

He turned deadly pale, and staggered against a tree, which alone prevented him from falling.

"It is true!" he gasped. "We are undone! The enemy is without doubt close at hand, and all is over. Yet," he added with more firmness, and with an appealing glance at the princess, "yet there may be one chance left for us. If this gracious lady will consent to go forward, instead of returning through the wood, we may yet escape with our lives. Noble princess!" and here he and the whole band assumed attitudes of supplication, "consider, I pray you, whether it would really add to your happiness to betray to the advancing army a few poor foresters, who earn their bread by the sweat of their brow. Here," he continued, hastily drawing something from a hole in the oak-tree, "is a bag containing ten thousand sapphires, each as large as a pullet's egg. If you will graciously deign to accept them, and to pursue your journey in the direction I shall indicate, the Red Chief of the Rustywhanger will be your slave forever."

The princess, who of course knew that there was no army in the neighborhood, and who moreover did not in the least care which way she went, assented to the Red Chief's proposition, and taking the bag of sapphires, bowed her farewell to the grateful robbers, and followed their leader down a ferny path which led to the farther end of the forest. When they came to the open country, the robber chieftain took his leave of the princess, with profound bows and many protestations of devotion, and returned to his band, who were already preparing to plunge into the impenetrable thickets of the midforest.

The princess, meantime, with her two bags of gems on her shoulders, fared forward with a light heart, by dale and by down, through moss and through meadow. By-and-by she came to a fair high palace, built all of marble and shining jasper, with smooth lawns about it, and sunny gardens of roses and gillyflowers, from which the air blew so sweet that it was a pleasure to breathe it. The princess stood still for a moment, to taste the sweetness of this air, and to look her fill at so fair a spot; and as she stood there, it chanced that the palace-gates opened, and the young king rode out with his court, to go a-catching of nighthawks.

Now when the king saw a right fair princess standing alone at his palace-gate, her rich garments dusty and travel-stained, and two heavy sacks hung upon her shoulders, he was filled with amazement; and leaping from his steed, like the gallant knight that he was, he besought her to tell him whence she came and whither she was going, and in what way he might be of service to her.

But the princess looked down at her little dusty shoes, and answered never a word; for she had seen at the first glance how fair and goodly a king this was, and she would not ask him the price of butter, nor whether his grandmother had sold her mangle yet. But she thought in her heart, "Now, I have never, in all my life, seen a man to whom I would so willingly say, 'With all my heart!' if he should ask me to marry him."

The king marvelled much at her silence, and presently repeated his questions, adding, "And what do you carry so carefully in those two sacks, which seem over-heavy for your delicate shoulders?"

Still holding her eyes downcast, the princess took a ruby from one bag, and a sapphire from the other, and in silence handed them to the king, for she willed that he should know she was no beggar, even though her shoes were dusty.

Thereat all the nobles were filled with amazement, for no such gems had ever been seen in that country.

But the king looked steadfastly at the princess, and said, "Rubies are fine, and sapphires are fair; but, maiden, if I could but see those eyes of yours, I warrant that the gems would look pale and dull beside them."

At that the princess raised her clear dark eyes, and looked at the king and smiled; and the glance of her eyes pierced straight to his heart, so that he fell on his knees and cried:

"Ah! sweet princess, now do I know that thou art the love for whom I have waited so long, and whom I have sought through so many lands. Give me thy white hand, and tell me, either by word or by sign, that thou wilt be my queen and my bride!"

And the princess, like a right royal maiden as she was, looked him straight in the eyes, and giving him her little white hand, answered bravely, "*With all my heart!*"

HOKEY POKEY

OKEY POKEY was the youngest of a large family of children. His elder brothers, as they grew up, all became either butchers or bakers or makers of candlesticks, for such was the custom of the family. But Hokey Pokey would be none of these things; so when he was grown to be a tall youth he went to his father and said, "Give me my fortune."

"'Will you be a butcher?' asked his father.

"'No,' said Hokey Pokey.

"'Will you be a baker?'

"'No, again.'

"'Will you make candlesticks?'

"'Nor that either.'

"'Then,' said his father, 'this is the only fortune I can give you;' and with that he took up his cudgel and gave the youth a stout beating. 'Now you cannot complain that I gave you nothing,' said he.

"'That is true,' said Hokey Pokey. 'But give me also the wooden mallet which lies on the shelf, and I will make my way through the world.'

"His father gave him the mallet, glad to be so easily rid of him, and Hokey Pokey went out into the world to seek his fortune. He walked all day, and at nightfall he came to a small village. Feeling hungry, he went into a baker's shop, intending to buy a loaf of bread for his supper. There was a great noise and confusion in the back part of the shop; and on going to see what was the matter, he found the baker on his knees beside a large box or chest, which he was trying with might and main to keep shut. But there was something inside the box which was trying just as hard to get out, and it screamed and kicked, and pushed the lid up as often as the baker shut it down.

"'What have you there in the box?' asked Hokey Pokey.

"'I have my wife,' replied the baker. 'She is so frightfully ill-tempered that whenever I am going to bake bread I am obliged to shut her up in this box, lest she push me into the oven and bake me with the bread, as she has often threatened to do. But to-day she has broken the lock of the box, and I know not how to keep her down.'

"'That is easily managed,' said Hokey Pokey. 'Do you but tell her, when she asks who I am, that I am a giant with three heads, and all will be well.' So saying, he took his wooden mallet and dealt three tremendous blows on the box, saying in a loud voice,—

'Hickory Hox!I sit by the box,Waiting to give you a few of my knocks.'

"'Husband, husband! whom have you there?' cried the wife in terror.

"'Alas!' said the baker; 'it is a frightful giant with three heads. He is sitting by the box, and if you open it so much as the width of your little finger, he will pull you out and beat you to powder.'

"When the wife heard that she crouched down in the box, and said never a word, for she was afraid of her life.

"The baker then took Hokey Pokey into the other part of the shop, thanked him warmly, and gave him a good supper and a bed. The next morning he gave him for a present the finest loaf of bread in his shop, which was shaped like a large round ball; and Hokey Pokey, after knocking once more on the lid of the box, continued his travels.

"He had not gone far before he came to another village, and wishing to inquire his way he entered the first shop he came to, which proved to be that of a confectioner. The shop was full of the most beautiful sweetmeats imaginable, and everything was bright and gay; but the confectioner himself sat upon a bench, weeping bitterly.

"'What ails you, friend?' asked Hokey Pokey; 'and why do you weep, when you are surrounded by the most delightful things in the world?'

"'Alas!' replied the confectioner. 'That is just the cause of my trouble. The sweetmeats that I make are so good that their fame has spread far and wide, and the Rat King, hearing of them, has taken up his abode in my cellar. Every night he comes up and eats all the sweetmeats I have made the day before. There is no comfort in my life, and I am thinking of becoming a rope-maker and hanging myself with the first rope I make.'

"'Why don't you set a trap for him?' asked Hokey Pokey.

"'I have set fifty-nine traps,' replied the confectioner, 'but he is so strong that he breaks them all.'

"'Poison him,' suggested Hokey Pokey.

"'He dislikes poison,' said the confectioner, 'and will not take it in any form.'

"'In that case,' said Hokey Pokey, 'leave him to me. Go away, and hide yourself for a few minutes, and all will be well.'

"The confectioner retired behind a large screen, having first showed Hokey Pokey the hole of the Rat King, which was certainly a very large one. Hokey

Pokey sat down by the hole, with his mallet in his hand, and said in a squeaking voice,—

'Ratly King! Kingly Rat!Here your mate comes pit-a-pat.Come and see; the way is free;Hear my signal: one! two! three!'

And he scratched three times on the floor. Almost immediately the head of a rat popped up through the hole. He was a huge rat, quite as large as a cat; but his size was no help to him, for as soon as he appeared, Hokey Pokey dealt him such a blow with his mallet that he fell down dead without even a squeak. Then Hokey Pokey called the confectioner, who came out from behind the screen and thanked him warmly; he also bade him choose anything he liked in the shop, in payment for his services.

"'Can you match this?' asked Hokey Pokey, showing his round ball of bread.

"'That can I!' said the confectioner; and he brought out a most beautiful ball, twice as large as the loaf, composed of the finest sweetmeats in the world, red and yellow and white. Hokey Pokey took it with many thanks, and then went on his way.

"The next day he came to a third village in the streets of which the people were all running to and fro in the wildest confusion.

"'What is the matter?' asked Hokey Pokey, as one man ran directly into his arms.

"'Alas!' replied the man. 'A wild bull has got into the principal china-shop, and is breaking all the beautiful dishes.'

"'Why do you not drive him out?' asked Hokey Pokey.

"'We are afraid to do that,' said the man; 'but we are running up and down to express our emotion and sympathy, and that is something.'

"'Show me the china-shop,' said Hokey Pokey.

"So the man showed him the china-shop; and there, sure enough, was a furious bull, making most terrible havoc. He was dancing up and down on a Dresden dinner set, and butting at the Chinese mandarins, and switching down finger-bowls and teapots with his tail, bellowing meanwhile in the most outrageous manner. The floor was covered with broken crockery, and the whole scene was melancholy to behold.

"Now when Hokey Pokey saw this, he said to the owner of the china-shop, who was tearing his hair in a frenzy of despair, 'Stop tearing your hair, which is indeed a senseless occupation, and I will manage this matter for you. Bring me a red cotton umbrella, and all will yet be well.'

"So the china-shop man brought him a red cotton umbrella, and Hokey Pokey began to open and shut it violently in front of the door. When the bull saw that, he stopped dancing on the Dresden dinner set and came charging out of the shop, straight towards the red umbrella. When he came near enough, Hokey Pokey dropped the umbrella, and raising his wooden mallet hit the bull such a blow on the muzzle that he fell down dead, and never bellowed again.

"The people all flung up their hats, and cheered, and ran up and down all the more, to express their gratification. As for the china-shop man, he threw his arms round Hokey Pokey's neck, called him his cherished preserver, and bade him choose anything that was left in his shop in payment for his services.

"'Can you match these?' asked Hokey Pokey, holding up the loaf of bread and the ball of sweetmeats.

"'That can I,' said the shop-man; and he brought out a huge ball of solid ivory, inlaid with gold and silver, and truly lovely to behold. It was very heavy, being twice as large as the ball of sweetmeats; but Hokey Pokey took it, and, after thanking the shop-man and receiving his thanks in return, he proceeded on his way.

"After walking for several days, he came to a fair, large castle, in front of which sat a man on horseback. When the man saw Hokey Pokey, he called out,—

"'Who are you, and what do you bring to the mighty Dragon, lord of this castle?'

"'Hokey Pokey is my name,' replied the youth, 'and strange things do I bring. But what does the mighty Dragon want, for example?'

"'He wants something new to eat,' said the man on horseback. 'He has eaten of everything that is known in the world, and pines for something new. He who brings him a new dish, never before tasted by him, shall have a thousand crowns and a new jacket; but he who fails, after three trials, shall have his jacket taken away from him, and his head cut off besides.'

"'I bring strange food,' said Hokey Pokey. 'Let me pass in, that I may serve the mighty Dragon.'

"Then the man on horseback lowered his lance, and let him pass in, and in short space he came before the mighty Dragon. The Dragon sat on a silver throne, with a golden knife in one hand, and a golden fork in the other. Around him were many people, who offered him dishes of every description; but he would none of them, for he had tasted them all before; and he howled with hunger on his silver throne. Then came forward Hokey Pokey, and said boldly,—

"'Here come I, Hokey Pokey, bringing strange food for the mighty Dragon.'

"The Dragon howled again, and waving his knife and fork, bade Hokey Pokey give the food to the attendants, that they might serve him.

"'Not so,' said Hokey Pokey. 'I must serve you myself, most mighty Dragon, else you shall not taste of my food. Therefore put down your knife and fork, and open your mouth, and you shall see what you shall see.'

"So the Dragon, after summoning the man-with-the-thousand-crowns and the man-with-the-new-jacket to one side of his throne, and the man-to-take-away-the old-jacket and the executioner to the other, laid down his knife and fork and opened his mouth. Hokey Pokey stepped lightly forward, and dropped the round loaf down the great red throat. The Dragon shut his jaws together with a snap, and swallowed the loaf in two gulps.

"'That is good,' he said; 'but it is not new. I have eaten much bread, though never before in a round loaf. Have you anything more? Or shall the man take away your jacket?'

"'I have this, an it please you,' said Hokey Pokey; and he dropped the ball of sweetmeats into the Dragon's mouth.

"When the Dragon tasted this, he rolled his eyes round and round, and was speechless with delight for some time. At length he said, 'Worthy youth, this is very good; it is extremely good; it is better than anything I ever tasted. Nevertheless, it is not new; for I have tasted the same kind of thing before, only not nearly so good. And now, unless you are positively sure that you have something new for your third trial, you really might as well take off your jacket; and the executioner shall take off your head at the same time, as it is getting rather late. Executioner, do your—'

"'Craving your pardon, most mighty Dragon,' said Hokey Pokey, 'I will first make my third trial;' and with that he dropped the ivory ball into the Dragon's mouth.

"'Gug-wugg-gllll-grrr!' said the Dragon, for the ball had stuck fast, being too big for him to swallow.

"Then Hokey Pokey lifted his mallet and struck one tremendous blow upon the ball, driving it far down the throat of the monster, and killing him most fatally dead. He rolled off the throne like a scaly log, and his crown fell off and rolled to Hokey Pokey's feet. The youth picked it up and put it on his own head, and then called the people about him and addressed them.

"'People,' he said, 'I am Hokey Pokey, and I have come from a far land to rule over you. Your Dragon have I slain, and now I am your king; and if you will always do exactly what I tell you to do, you will have no further trouble.'

"So the people threw up their caps and cried, 'Long live Hokey Pokey!' and they always did exactly as he told them, and had no further trouble.

"And Hokey Pokey sent for his three brothers, and made them Chief Butcher, Chief Baker, and Chief Candlestick-maker of his kingdom. But to his father he sent a large cudgel made of pure gold, with these words engraved on it: 'Now you cannot complain that I have given you nothing!'"

THE TANGLED SKEIN

Y dear child," said the Angel-who-attends-to things, "why are you crying so very hard?"

"Oh dear! oh dear!" said the child. "No one ever had such a dreadful time before, I do believe, and it all comes of trying to be good. Oh dear! Oh dear! I wish I was bad; then I should not have all this trouble."

"Yes, you would," said the Angel; "a great deal worse. Now tell me what is the matter!"

"Look!" said the child. "Mother gave me this skein to wind, and I promised to do it. But then father sent me on an errand, and it was almost school-time, and I was studying my lesson and going on the errand and winding the skein, all at the same time, and now I have got all tangled up in the wool, and I cannot walk either forward or back, and oh! dear me, what ever *shall* I do?"

"Sit down!" said the Angel.

"But it is school-time!" said the child.

"Sit down!" said the Angel.

"But father sent me on an errand!" said the child.

"SIT DOWN!" said the Angel; and he took the child by her shoulders and set her down.

"Now sit still!" he said, and he began patiently to wind up the skein. It was wofully tangled, and knotted about the child's hands and feet; it was a wonder she could move at all; but at last it was all clear, and the Angel handed her the ball.

"I thank you so very much!" said the child. "I was not naughty, was I?"

"Not naughty, only foolish; but that does just as much harm sometimes."

"But I was doing right things!" said the child.

"But you were doing them in the wrong way!" said the Angel. "It is good to do an errand, and it is good to go to school, but when you have a skein to wind you must sit still."

A SONG FOR HAL

NCE I saw a little boat, and a pretty, pretty boat,
When daybreak the hills was adorning,
And into it I jumped, and away I did float,
So very, very early in the morning.

Chorus

And every little wave had its nightcap on,
Its nightcap, white cap, nightcap on.
And every little wave had its nightcap on,
So very, very early in the morning.

All the fishes were asleep in their caves cool and deep,
When the ripple round my keel flashed a warning.
Said the minnow to the skate, "We must certainly be late,
Though I thought 't was very early in the morning."

Chorus

For every little wave has its nightcap on,
Its nightcap, white cap, nightcap on.
For every little wave has its nightcap on,
So very, very early in the morning.

The lobster darkly green soon appeared upon the scene,
And pearly drops his claws were adorning.
Quoth he, "May I be boiled, if I'll have my slumber spoiled,
So very, very early in the morning!"

Chorus

For every little wave has its nightcap on,
Its nightcap, white cap, nightcap on,
For every little wave has its nightcap on,
So very, very early in the morning.

Said the sturgeon to the eel, "Just imagine how I feel,
Thus roused without a syllable of warning.
People ought to let us know when a-sailing they would go,

So very, very early in the morning."

Chorus

When every little wave has its nightcap on,
Its nightcap, white cap, nightcap on.
When every little wave has its nightcap on,
So very, very early in the morning.

Just then up jumped the sun, and the fishes every one
For their laziness at once fell a-mourning.
But I stayed to hear no more, for my boat had reached the shore,
So very, very early in the morning.

Chorus

And every little wave took its nightcap off,
Its nightcap, white cap, nightcap off.
And every little wave took its nightcap off,
And courtesied to the sun in the morning.

HAVE come to speak to you about your work," said the Angel-who-attends-to-things. "It appears to be unsatisfactory."

"Indeed!" said the man. "I hardly see how that can be. Perhaps you will explain."

"I will!" said the Angel. "To begin with, the work is slovenly."

"I was born heedless," said the man. "It is a family failing which I have always regretted."

"It is ill put together, too;" said the Angel. "The parts do not fit."

"I never had any eye for proportion," said the man; "I admit it is unfortunate."

"The whole thing is a botch," said the Angel. "You have put neither brains nor heart into it, and the result is ridiculous failure. What do you propose to do about it?"

"I credited you with more comprehension," said the man. "My faults, such as they are, were born with me. I am sorry that you do not approve of me, but this is the way I was made; do you see?"

"I see!" said the Angel. He put out a strong white hand, and taking the man by the collar, tumbled him neck and crop into the ditch.

"What is the meaning of this?" cried the man, as he scrambled out breathless and dripping. "I never saw such behavior. Do you see what you have done? you have ruined my clothes, and nearly drowned me beside."

"Oh yes!" said the Angel: "this is the way *I* was made."

THE BURNING HOUSE

OME neighbours were walking together in the cool of the day, watching the fall of the twilight, and talking of this and that; and as they walked, they saw at a little distance a light, as it were a house on fire.

"From the direction, that must be our neighbour William's house," said one. "Ought we not to warn him of the danger?"

"I see only a little flame," said another; "perchance it may go out of itself, and no harm done."

"I should be loth to carry ill news," said a third; "it is always a painful thing to do."

"William is not a man who welcomes interference," said a fourth. "I should not like to be the one to intrude upon his privacy; probably he knows about the fire, and is managing it in his own way."

While they were talking, the house burned up.

THE NAUGHTY COMET

HE door of the Comet House was open. In the great court-yard stood hundreds of comets, of all sizes and shapes. Some were puffing and blowing, and arranging their tails, all ready to start; others had just come in, and looked shabby and forlorn after their long journeyings, their tails drooping disconsolately; while others still were switched off on side-tracks, where the tinker and the tailor were attending to their wants, and setting them to rights. In the midst of all stood the Comet Master, with his hands behind him, holding a very long stick with a very sharp point. The comets knew just how the point of that stick felt, for they were prodded with it whenever they misbehaved themselves; accordingly, they all remained very quiet, while he gave his orders for the day.

In a distant corner of the court-yard lay an old comet, with his tail comfortably curled up around him. He was too old to go out, so he enjoyed himself at home in a quiet way. Beside him stood a very young comet, with a very short tail. He was quivering with excitement, and occasionally cast sharp impatient glances at the Comet Master.

"Will he *never* call me?" he exclaimed, but in an undertone, so that only his companion could hear. "He knows I am dying to go out, and for that very reason he pays no attention to me. I dare not leave my place, for you know what he is."

"Ah!" said the old comet, slowly, "if you had been out as often as I have, you would not be in such a hurry. Hot, tiresome work, *I* call it. And what does it all amount to?"

"Ay, that's the point!" exclaimed the young comet. "What *does* it all amount to? That is what I am determined to find out. I cannot understand your going on, travelling and travelling, and never finding out why you do it. *I* shall find out, you may be very sure, before I have finished my first journey."

"Better not! better not!" answered the old comet. "You'll only get into trouble. Nobody knows except the Comet Master and the Sun. The Master would cut you up into inch pieces if you asked him, and the Sun—"

"Well, what about the Sun?" asked the young comet, eagerly.

"Short-tailed Comet No. !" rang suddenly, clear and sharp, through the court-yard.

The young comet started as if he had been shot, and in three bounds he stood before the Comet Master, who looked fixedly at him.

"You have never been out before," said the Master.

"No, sir!" replied No. ; and he knew better than to add another word.

"You will go out now," said the Comet Master. "You will travel for thirteen weeks and three days, and will then return. You will avoid the neighborhood of the Sun, the Earth, and the planet Bungo. You will turn to the left on meeting other comets, and you are not allowed to speak to meteors. These are your orders. Go!"

At the word, the comet shot out of the gate and off into space, his short tail bobbing as he went.

Ah! here was something worth living for. No longer shut up in that tiresome court-yard, waiting for one's tail to grow, but out in the free, open, boundless realm of space, with leave to shoot about here and there and everywhere— well, *nearly* everywhere—for thirteen whole weeks! Ah, what a glorious prospect! How swiftly he moved! How well his tail looked, even though it was still rather short! What a fine fellow he was, altogether!

For two or three weeks our comet was the happiest creature in all space; too happy to think of anything except the joy of frisking about. But by-and-by he began to wonder about things, and that is always dangerous for a comet.

"I wonder, now," he said, "why I may not go near the planet Bungo. I have always heard that he was the most interesting of all the planets. And the Sun! how I *should* like to know a little more about the Sun! And, by the way, that reminds me that all this time I have never found out *why* I am travelling. It shows how I have been enjoying myself, that I have forgotten it so long; but now I must certainly make a point of finding out. Hello! there comes Long-Tail No. . I mean to ask him."

So he turned out to the left, and waited till No. came along. The latter was a middle-aged comet, very large, and with an uncommonly long tail,—quite preposterously long, our little No. thought, as he shook his own tail and tried to make as much of it as possible.

"Good morning, Mr. Long-Tail!" he said as soon as the other was within speaking distance. "Would you be so very good as to tell me what you are travelling for?"

"For six months," answered No. with a puff and a snort. "Started a month ago; five months still to go."

"Oh, I don't mean that!" exclaimed Short-Tail No. . "I mean *why* are you travelling at all?"

"Comet Master sent me!" replied No. , briefly.

"But what for?" persisted the little comet. "What is it all about? What good does it do? *Why* do we travel for weeks and months and years? That's what I want to find out."

"Don't know, I'm sure!" said the elder, still more shortly. "What's more, don't care!"

The little comet fairly shook with amazement and indignation. "You don't care!" he cried. "Is it possible? And how long, may I ask, have you been travelling hither and thither through space, without knowing or caring why?"

"Long enough to learn not to ask stupid questions!" answered Long-Tail No. . "Good morning to you!"

And without another word he was off, with his preposterously long tail spreading itself like a luminous fan behind him. The little comet looked after him for some time in silence. At last he said:—

"Well, *I* call that simply *disgusting*! An ignorant, narrow-minded old—"

"Hello, cousin!" called a clear merry voice just behind him. "How goes it with you? Shall we travel together? Our roads seem to go in the same direction."

The comet turned and saw a bright and sparkling meteor. "I—I—must not speak to you!" said No. , confusedly.

"Not speak to me!" exclaimed the meteor, laughing. "Why, what's the matter? What have I done? I never saw you before in my life."

"N-nothing that I know of," answered No. , still more confused.

"Then why mustn't you speak to me?" persisted the meteor, giving a little skip and jump. "Eh? tell me that, will you? *Why* mustn't you?"

"I—don't—know!" answered the little comet, slowly, for he was ashamed to say boldly, as he ought to have done, that it was against the orders of the Comet Master.

"Oh, gammon!" cried the meteor, with another skip. "*I* know! Comet Master, eh? But a fine high-spirited young fellow like you isn't going to be afraid of that old tyrant. Come along, I say! If there were any *real reason* why you should not speak to me—"

"That's just what I say," interrupted the comet, eagerly. "What IS the reason? Why don't they tell it to me?"

"'Cause there isn't any!" rejoined the meteor. "Come along!"

After a little more hesitation, the comet yielded, and the two frisked merrily along, side by side. As they went, No. confided all his vexations to his new friend, who sympathized warmly with him, and spoke in most disrespectful terms of the Comet Master.

"A pretty sort of person to dictate to you, when he hasn't the smallest sign of a tail himself! I wouldn't submit to it!" cried the meteor. "As to the other orders, some of them are not so bad. Of course, nobody would want to go near that stupid, poky Earth, if he could possibly help it; and the planet Bungo is—ah—is not a very nice planet, I believe." The fact is, the planet Bungo contains a large reform-school for unruly meteors, but our friend made no mention of that. "But as for the Sun,—the bright, jolly, delightful Sun,—why, I am going to take a nearer look at him myself. Come on! We will go together, in spite of the Comet Master."

Again the little comet hesitated and demurred; but after all, he had already broken one rule, and why not another? He would be punished in any case, and he might as well get all the pleasure he could. Reasoning thus, he yielded once more to the persuasions of the meteor, and together they shot through the great space-world, taking their way straight toward the Sun.

When the Sun saw them coming, he smiled and seemed much pleased. He stirred his fire, and shook his shining locks, and blazed brighter and brighter, hotter and hotter. The heat seemed to have a strange effect on the comet, for he began to go faster and faster.

"Hold on!" said the meteor. "Why are you hurrying so? I cannot keep up with you."

"I cannot stop myself!" cried No. . "Something is drawing me forward, faster and faster!"

On he went at a terrible rate, the meteor following as best he might. Several planets that he passed shouted to him in warning tones, but he could not hear what they said. The Sun stirred his fire again, and blazed brighter and brighter, hotter and hotter; and onward rushed the wretched little comet, faster and faster, faster and faster!

"Catch hold of my tail and stop me!" he shrieked to the meteor. "I am shrivelling, burning up, in this fearful heat! Stop me, for pity's sake!"

But the meteor was already far behind, and had stopped short to watch his companion's headlong progress. And now,—ah, me!—now the Sun opened his huge fiery mouth. The comet made one desperate effort to stop himself, but it was in vain. An awful, headlong plunge through the intervening space; a hissing and crackling; a shriek,—and the fiery jaws had closed on Short-Tail No. forever!

"Dear me!" said the meteor. "How very shocking! I quite forgot that the Sun ate comets. I must be off, or I shall get an æon in the Reform School for this. I am really very sorry, for he was a nice little comet!"

And away frisked the meteor, and soon forgot all about it.

But in the great court-yard in front of the Comet House, the Master took a piece of chalk, and crossed out No. from the list of short-tailed comets on the slate that hangs on the door. Then he called out, "No. Express, come forward!" and the swiftest of all the comets stood before him, brilliant and beautiful, with a bewildering magnificence of tail. The Comet Master spoke sharply and decidedly, as usual, but not unkindly.

"No. , Short-Tail," he said, "has disobeyed orders, and has in consequence been devoured by the Sun."

Here there was a great sensation among the comets.

"No. ," continued the Master, "you will start immediately, and travel until you find a runaway meteor, with a red face and blue hair. You are permitted to make inquiries of respectable bodies, such as planets or satellites. When found, you will arrest him and take him to the planet Bungo. My compliments to the Meteor Keeper, and I shall be obliged if he will give this meteor two æons in the Reform School. I trust," he continued, turning to the assembled comets, "that this will be a lesson to all of you!"

And I believe it was.

DAY DREAMS

HITE wings over the water,
Fluttering, fluttering over the sea,
White wings over the water,
What are you bringing to me?
A fairy prince in a golden boat,
With golden ringlets that fall and float,
A velvet cap, and a taffety cloak,
This you are bringing to me.

Fairy, fairy princekin,
Sailing, sailing hither to me,
Silk and satin and velvet,
What are you coming to see?
A little girl in a calico gown,
With hair and eyes of dusky brown,
Who sits on the wharf of the fishing-town.

Golden, golden sunbeams,
Touch me now with your wands of gold;
Make me a beautiful princess,
Radiant to behold.
Blue and silver and ermine fine,
Diamond drops that flash and shine;
So shall I meet this prince of mine,
Fairer than may be told.

White wings over the water,
Fluttering ever farther away;
Dark clouds shrouding the sunbeams,
Sullen and cold and gray.
Back I go in my calico gown,
Back to the hut in the fishing-town.
And oh, but the night shuts darkly down
After the summer day!